Room 9

Room 9
by Clifford Beck

For My Brother, Randy

Copyright©2022Clifford Beck
Cover design – Clifford Beck

1

The school day at Deering High School started much like any other, with students scurrying to their assigned homerooms, trying to avoid being late. But this day was different and held the promise of changing the lives of a small handful of gifted youths, those bound for more than ordinary careers. Their focus was on the sciences, and they would soon be off for a one-week tour of Nasa's Langley Research Center in Hampton, Virginia, generously paid for by the Department of Education. Those with the highest grades had their names entered in a lottery, with the first five winners being the ones chosen.

The first was Chelsea, a senior who had just been accepted to Harvard Medical College. She had already been taking college-level classes in medical biology and anatomy. Her parents managed to avoid the burden of paying her tuition when she was offered a full scholarship for as long as she attended in her chosen field. The second was John, a promising engineering student who arrived from Italy with his parents when he was merely four years old. For the sake of fitting in, his parent decided to change his name, believing that he would be less of a target for those who might harass him. The third winner was Kyle, who was seen by many as the class clown. His sense of humor sometimes got in the way of classroom order, and many of his teachers wondered if he had a future at all should he be expelled. To avoid such a fate, he was given a lot of chances to correct his conduct, perhaps too many. But he believed himself to be above the rules and repeatedly displayed a noticeable arrogance that left others talking about him behind his back, using words such as high school students tend to use. However, as a gifted teen, his genius lay in nuclear chemistry, and he had already been contacted by the Department of Defense. The fourth in line was Kate, a passionate artist with a special gift for aerospace design. Having already produced several designs, the school sent them off to Nasa where they were quickly acquired by the military and deemed classified. Never having had a boyfriend, there were those who questioned her sexuality based, in part, on her boyish looks. This, however, was of no concern to her, as she was quite comfortable with who she was and had better things to do than worry about what others thought of her. Lastly, there was Ethan, bound for MIT's mechanical engineering program. As a small boy, he was curious about anything that had moving parts and promptly disassembled them. While once taking apart the gears of a small music box, he thought he might try to force one into its opposite direction using his teeth. However, when his teeth slipped against it his bottom lip quickly became lodged between it and its opposing cog, cutting into his flesh and by his shrieks, attracted the attention of his parents. With the right tools, Ethan's father removed his bleeding lip from the brass gears and, applying pressure, rushed him to the hospital. One might think this would have been the end of his fascination with all things mechanical. But strangely, Ethan found himself even more curious, and it was this that propelled him into engineering, standing at the doorway of a brilliant college career at one of the country's most prestigious universities.

Their parents were thrilled, knowing that the success of their children would favorably reflect on them in the eyes of the community. But even the parents could not anticipate what was waiting for them at the Langley Research Center as the group of teens toured the vast technological arm of the government. Some things happen by intent, while others are brought on by ignorance. What would happen at

Langley would be brought about by both in equal measure, bringing a sudden halt to the youth's promising future.

2

With the student body packed into Deering High School's auditorium, the five teens were brought up on stage as their fellow student applauded with excitement. Although there were some who were not chosen and maintained an obvious degree of jealousy, as is usually the case for those seen as 'sore losers'. But for the most part, the small group's departure was recognized as a time of celebration as they prepared for what they considered to be a once in a lifetime adventure. Naturally, according to school policy, the small group was to have an adult in attendance and with the teachers busy delivering their lessons it was decided that a parent should go. Without hesitation, Kate's mother, Elaine, stepped up to volunteer, having always admired her daughter's artwork. Now, she would get to glimpse the path of Kate's future and was quite eager for the group to be their way. Perhaps more than the teens themselves. Unlike most teenagers, Kate was happy to have her mother alone for the trip, having, at times, experienced her relationship with her as more than simply parental. One might say that they occasionally seemed to be friends. However, Kate's mother had the last say in any disagreement.

3

Teenagers are not generally known for rising early but today was an exception as their flight out of Portland International was scheduled for eight o'clock they were forced to rise at five in the morning. As is typical, they complained the entire way to the airport. But Kate's mother reminded them of the rare opportunity waiting for them at the end of their trip, and after boarding the plane, the group quickly fell asleep, including Kate's mother. However, their slumber was broken by the plane's wheels as they touched down in Boston, accompanied by the whining of rapidly slowing engines. Still drowsy, the group slowly disembarked and walked the short distance to the terminal. Kate was the first to ask.

"Are we there yet?"

Her voice was groggy and her eyes bloodshot. Aircraft seats are not ordinarily used as beds, and the group was already feeling their lack of comfort.

"Not yet," her mother replied. "We're only in Boston. We've still got a ways to go yet."

Upon leaving the plane, Kate groaned in disappointment as she slowly found her way to the nearest chair. Her mother, however, was quick to interrupt her and directed her instructions to the entire group, now seated at the gate.

"Guys," she began. "This isn't our gate. C'mon, we gotta get going."

Ethan was the first to speak up.

"Can't we just sit here for a while? Just for a few minutes?"

Those who had not fallen asleep also groaned their displeasure at the idea of having to muster enough energy to walk

to the next gate.
"Do you guys want to go to NASA or not?" Elaine continued.

She expected a few minor issues from the teens and certainly, this would qualify, but missing their connecting flight was not an option. The only response from the group was the muffled grumbles of protest as they got to their feet. Grabbing their carry-on bags, they stammered to the next gate, where they promptly drifted off as soon as their back-sides hit the chairs. Half an hour went by before a loudspeaker blared out the call to board, and slowly the teens got to their feet, hurried by Elaine.
"C'mon guys," she said. "We gotta move."

Getting to their feet, they made their way to the check-in line with boarding passes in hand, trudging forward every few seconds with an expression of near coma glazed over their faces. But Elaine had managed to cheat the effects of sleep deprivation by quickly procuring a large cup of coffee, and with wakeful eyes she continued as the group's sentinel, making sure that everyone stayed together. Now, passing through check-in, the group boarded the plane and finding their seats put their carry-on baggage in the overhead compartments. None of them were awake long enough to hear the flight attendant's instructions, but they did remain awake long enough to fasten their seatbelts. The rest of the flight was spent deep in an exhausted sleep, broken only by the aircraft's bumpy landing.

4

Arriving at their destination, Elaine coordinated the groggy teens together and prompted them toward the front of the plane, where they disembarked. The gangway was loud with the sound of engines winding down, but warm with the fresh Virginia air. Arriving at the luggage carousel, she noticed a man standing near the hallway with a sign that read 'Nasa Tour Group'. It was only now that she realized that they had been assigned a driver and that she would not have to rent a car, as she had planned. With the group in tow, Elaine walked quickly to the well-dressed man and inquired as to his assignment.
"Are you here for the kids from Portland?"
The man nodded and answered promptly.
"Yes, ma'am, right this way".
Elaine turned to the group, their minds still lost in the haze of well-needed sleep.
"C'mon guys," she began. "Our ride is here."

The driver's hurried pace forced the group from a trudging walk to a stiff jog until finally leaving the terminal. Not far away was a gray van with the word 'NASA' boldly stenciled on its side. The driver was good enough to help put their luggage in the rear of the van as the group filed in. Once again, they dozed off as soon as they sat down. All but Elaine, who sat in the front still nursing her coffee, her eyes wide with the rush of caffeine.

5

The drive to Hampton seemed to take forever as the teens continued their drifting journey, gently cradled by the arms of Morpheus, their eyes darting from side-to-side while their minds reflected on the anticipation of what lay ahead. The driver wasn't much on conversation, but this left Elaine with the opportunity to see what she could of Virginia, mostly highways, overpasses, and office towers. This she found somewhat disappointing, as she expected to see rolling hills and dense forests, all the things typical of that part of the country. However, feeling a bit of tension from the absence of conversation, she tried to break the ice with a little small talk with the driver.
"So," she began. "How long have you been working for NASA?"
Elaine was a single mother and having just met such a well-built man who, surprisingly, also had a job, sent her into a hormonal spiral as she began to flush. But it was his voice that truly tested her impulses.
"Ma'am," he replied. "I've been with NASA for over ten years."

Elaine had not been involved with anyone for several years, ignoring her need for the company of a man while undertaking the raising of her daughter. Now, she felt that need spring to life with a vengeance and feeling the fiery flush of arousal opened the passenger window, allowing the breeze to cool her skin as well as the fire sweeping through her soul. But in spite of this, she continued the conversation. She simply could not get enough of what his voice did to her.

"So," she said. "Have you always done this for NASA? The driving, I mean?"

He made no eye contact and responded with a stiff, professional voice.

"Ma'am, I work in security. I just do what they tell me."

Elaine couldn't help feeling put off by his impersonal approach, but it also occurred to her that, given the nature of his job, maintaining an emotional distance was likely necessary. Yet, Elaine couldn't help trying one more time and left him with an open invitation.

"Well," she began. "If you're ever up in Maine, you'll have to stop by."

His professional demeanor was momentarily broken by a slight grin as he briefly responded to her advance.

"I'll be sure to remember, ma'am."

Leaving the highway, a Holiday Inn came into view and as Elaine's unusual hot flash broke she, again, turned to the driver.

"Is this where we're staying?" she asked.

"Yes, ma'am," he replied. "You're only a few miles from the research center."

As he pulled into the hotel parking lot, the driver, led by curiosity, inquired about their visit.

"So," he began. "If you don't mind me asking, what is it that brings you down here?"

Elaine turned back, informing the teens that they had arrived at their hotel.

"Well," she began. "The kids here won a lottery to spend a week touring the center. They're part of the school's gifted and talented program."

The driver nodded.

"A week, huh?" he asked. "I don't know, there's a lot to see

here. A week won't be enough time, but they'll probably get to see only certain things. Most of the projects are classified. The government does have to keep its secrets, ya know."
"Oh," Elaine replied. "Well, even if they can't see everything, I'm sure they'll have a good time anyway."
Suddenly feeling the importance of where they were going, she refrained from asking any more questions.

　　Pulling into a parking space, the driver got out and began unloading the group's luggage as the teens roused from their short sleep. Approaching Elaine, he began one more brief conversation.
"Ma'am, you'll be getting a wake-up call at seven in the morning. I'll pick you up at eight."
Elaine was pleasantly surprised and asked him if he would be driving them back and forth during the entire week. His answer was yes and as he drove away, she couldn't help thinking that maybe she had a chance for, at least, a brief reprieve from the years of loneliness she had experienced, even though she knew there would be no time for such an indulgence, and he likely wouldn't be interested anyway.

6

The evening passed uneventfully, with dinner ordered as soon as the group's luggage was stored. Elaine suggested a movie, but the teens decided that sleep was a bit more important. According to the rules laid down by the school, they were dividing into two rooms according to gender. Both privacy and personal conduct were seen as priorities. After all, they were representing their high school and the reputation of both their school and their character would be open to criticism. But for now, sleep was the only thing on their minds. Even Elaine, with the rush now wearing off, was beginning to feel the slight effects of jet lag and as soon as her head hit the pillow, she too drifted off into a deep sleep.

7

The alarm clock went off at five thirty in the morning and, as usual, the teens were slow to rise but eventually, mustered the energy to carry out the morning's ritual. Discovering that the hotel had a free continental breakfast, they quickly took advantage, filling their stomachs almost to capacity. However, there was one exception. Kate was quite a small-framed girl and was not accustomed to such large portions. The mere sight of her friends cramming their faces with what was, essentially junk food, nearly made her ill, but she managed to distract herself by turning away and engaging her mother in conversation.
"So, mom," she began. "What's up with you and the driver? You planning on getting lucky?"
Elaine had been under the impression that everyone had fallen asleep on the way over, and met Kate's curiosity with a bit of humor.
"Why?" she asked. "Do you think I should ask him out? Let me tell ya' something, kiddo, these double doors are almost rusted shut and I definitely need someone to pry them open."
Letting out a sigh of frustration, she quietly followed up with something that immediately closed the conversation.
"God, I'll bet he's got a huge dick."
Responding with embarrassment, Kate quickly brought her hands up over her flushed face.
"Jesus Christ, mom, not here! What is wrong with you?"
The one thing she didn't need to hear from her mother was anything about the male anatomy. Fortunately, she was the only person to hear her mother's remarks. Yet, it would

take her quite some time to get the conversation out of her head. Certainly, she would never bring up the issue of men again. At least, not with her mother.
"Hey," she said. "I have needs."
A last parting shot. If it was one thing Elaine had in abundance, it was a twisted sense of humor.

8

After breakfast, the group was once again whisked off to their destination. As they neared the front gate, all eyes grew wide with fascination as the vast complex of Nasa's campus quickly came into view. Even Kate's mother stopped gawking at the driver long enough to take in the sight of Nasa's vast technological array of buildings, antennae, and military vehicles. There were other vehicles that had been painted white with the words 'Homeland Security' emblazoned down each side. Taken together, the entire scene left the group feeling more than a bit intimidated, but also fully aware of the high level of secrecy that enshrouded everything within view. They also knew that there would be more.

9

Pulling up to the front entrance of the main building, the group disembarked, but was held in check by a small number of well-armed guards. After a few tense minutes, a well-dressed middle-aged man stepped out of the building and quickly approached the tour group.
"Good morning, everyone!"
In spite of the earliness of the day, he seemed rather chipper. Perhaps, he had drunk a bit too much coffee or was instructed to use an entertaining approach, given the age of the group.
"My name is Doctor Elijah Stewart, and I'll be showing you around this week."
Certainly, there were things he could be doing that actually met his qualifications. Yet, it was obvious he had been drafted for the task of supervising five teenagers in a place where most things were highly classified, and off-limits to all except those involved.
Kate raised her hand.
"Yes, miss, you have a question?" he asked.
"You used the word Doctor. What do you do here?"
He wasn't entirely surprised by her question. After all, these were highly gifted, intelligent teenagers and very prone to curiosity.
"Well," he began. "I am the head of the department of astrophysical engineering."
A confused look took over Kate's face as she continued with her questions.
"What does that mean?" she asked.
He paused for a moment to gather his words, trying not to

say anything that would reveal something of a classified nature.

"Well," he replied. "That's a good question."

Kate already felt patronized, but tried not to express her frustration.

"Most of the things we work on are very classified, but we focus our work on space travel."

Kate grew even more frustrated with only two words floating around in her head.

'No shit.'

The rest of the students were left in awe of their tour guide's transparent response, and did more than an exemplary job of containing their laughter. But as they entered the building, it was Kate's mother who turned toward the driver and, making eye contact, winked at him and blew him a kiss. Seeing this out of the corner of her eye, Kate turned and quietly snapped at her.

"Mom," she began. "How about a little self-control? Jesus Christ."

As they made their way to the elevators, Kate's mom made a weak attempt to deliver an excuse for her behavior.

"I'm sorry, hon," she began. "But I think I've been single for way too long, and that driver, holy shit."

At hearing this, Kate's frustration began to peak and, again, scolded her mother.

"Mom, will you just stop already? We're not here for this."

Her mother suddenly felt the flush of embarrassment and would spend the remainder of their tour in a quiet, self-conscious state.

Before the tour could get underway, there was a necessary formality in the way of paperwork. While the teens were still standing in the corridor, a sheet of printed paper was passed out to each of the teens, as well as Elaine.

"Okay," Doctor Stewart began. "These are non-disclosure agreements. You will not proceed any further on this campus without signing this agreement. What this says is that when your tour is over, you will not tell anyone about anything you saw here. Some of our projects and military related, and disclosing any information pertaining to them could become a threat to national security. Do you understand? The teens found the doctor's approach somewhat threatening, but they did understand the importance of secrecy where military research is concerned.

The signed paperwork was handed back, and the tour was on its way as Doctor Stewart led the group down the corridor. Reaching the elevator, he pushed the button for the third floor as a few of the teens seemed to tremble in anticipation. They were looking forward to seeing some tomorrow's technology.

10

The elevator car was spacious enough that everyone could enter without becoming crowded. After the doors closed, it was only a few brief moments before the elevator opened at the third floor. Having noticed skipping the second floor, Ethan brought it to the attention of their tour guide.
"Why didn't we stop at the second floor?"
Their guide was quick with an answer, albeit a necessary lie.
"The second floor is all administration," he replied.
The teenagers quickly believed his lie. Many times, on government facilities, secrecy was often the chosen weapon that protected the interests of the country, be it technology or the operation of organizations that don't exist on paper.

Stopping at the third floor, the elevator doors opened as the eyes of the five teenagers grew wide with excitement and curiosity. Their guide excused himself and walked through the open doors and, putting out a hand, led the teens out into a spacious corridor lined on both side with doors, whose windows were constructed of frosted glass. It was assumed by the group that these windows were designed specifically to keep prying eyes away from things that should not be seen.

Leading the group down the corridor, Doctor Stewart took them to an area dedicated to engineering. While opening the door, he instructed the students to stand against the wall so as not to be in the way. Once this was accomplished, he motioned over to where work was being done on a rather unusual device.

"Now," he began. "Over here, we're currently working on what we call the 'quantum engine' and…"

"I've read about that," Ethan interrupted.

The group turned to him, waiting for him to elaborate.

"It's basically a thruster engine that doesn't need liquid fuel, so it runs on electricity. I'm still not sure how it works, but that's basically it."

Doctor Stewart thought carefully as he studied his face. He knew there would be a risk of contamination, but he wanted to make some small contribution, and perhaps provide a bit of inspiration to what he saw as the mind of a genius.

"Ethan," he began. "How would you like to get a closer look?"

Ethan's eyes grew wide with excitement at the prospect of standing that close to a form of technology he could not possibly begin to understand.

"Are you kidding?!" he replied. "You mean, now?"

Seeing the broad smile overtake Ethan's face, Doctor Stewart knew he had made the right decision, but Ethan would have to be briefed first. The other four teens were left speechless as he was led around a corner and through a door painted with the words 'Classified – Staff Only.'

He was led to a modest room whose purpose was for the preparation of those working with the engine. They were required to wash their hands and face thoroughly and dress in a white one-piece protective suit. It was not designed so much for their protection but to avoid contaminating the engine as well as the tools used in its construction. Ten minutes later, Ethan and the doctor emerged from a back entrance and circled around to where the engineering staff was huddled about what could be seen as impossible technology. Of course, his fellow students had gathered at the window, their eyes glued to the sight of Ethan being motioned closer to the engine while the chief engineer explained its inner workings. Although most of the information was difficult for him to understand, this only served to pique his curiosity. After another ten minutes, Ethan, along with Doctor Stewart, emerged into the corridor to the congratulatory cheers of the group. Even Kate's mother was more than impressed.

Order was soon brought to the group of excited teen as Doctor Stewart lead them to their stop. This time it would be Chelsea who would lead into a specialized area dedicated to medical research.
"Now," Doctor Stewart began. "Our next stop is two floors up. So, if you will all follow me."
The group followed closely behind, but it was their curiosity that propelled them forward. With the elevator doors closing in front of them, the doctor pushed a glowing yellow button, sending them several floors up. When they stepped off, they were again led down a long corridor, stopping in front of, yet, another door. They all seemed to look the same and could cause one to easily become lost amidst the vast catacombs of technology and classified areas.
"Okay," the doctor said. He turned his attention towards Chelsea. "In this area, we're working on several medical projects."

As tired as she was, Chelsea face came to life with excitement as she wondered if she would be next to get up close to the leading technology in medical research. Aside from the development of space technology reserved for astronauts, this department was also working on projects for commercial use, including smaller fiber-optic scopes for use in joint surgery, as well as advanced heart pumps.
"So, Chelsea," he continued. "I've heard that you're the

one who's going to Harvard Medical school. How would you like a tour of the department?"

Chelsea nearly jumped out of her skin, throwing herself at the doctor and hugging him tightly.

"Oh my God!" she replied. "You have no idea!"

Once she became aware of her behavior, her face flushed with embarrassment as she released her grip on the doctor and stepped back.

"I'm sorry," she said. "I didn't mean to…"

The doctor, understanding the exuberant nature of adolescence, reassured Chelsea that no offense was taken. Leading her around a nearby corner, Chelsea found herself in what had been dubbed 'a clean room'. She was instructed to put on a clean white suit over her clothes and was assisted by a senior staff member in sealing the cuffs around both her wrists and ankles. After putting a protective hood, the technician put a belt around her waist and turned on a battery operated filter that connected to the back of the hood. As the sound of the filter's motor whirred in her ears, she was led into the lab, where she gasped in wonder at what she would later describe as miracles of science.

The doctor motioned her over to a Plexiglas box. As she looked in that direction, Chelsea was stunned to find a human heart beating with almost perfect regularity. But something was different. And as she got closer, she became in awe of what was being done to this object. What would ordinarily be a complex system of striated muscles appeared as a grouping of transparent leaves that had been attached to each other in the shape of a heart. Yet, it was beating.

"So," the doctor began. "What do you make of this?"

Chelsea had recently written a paper on decellularization and was moderately familiar with the technology being used for this particular project.

"So," she replied. "You finally did it."

The doctor seemed perplexed as her familiarity with what she was seeing.

"You know something about this?" he asked.

"Well," she continued. "Without the cells, you can engineer a heart from stem cells and infuse the cell matrix with them. As long as they get the right nutrients, you should end up with functioning striated muscle. Its electrical system should form on its own. But I don't see this going into commercial use for at least ten years, and then there's FDA approval."

Doctor Stewart realized he should not be surprised at how much the teens knew about this advanced level of science, but he couldn't help being taken aback by Chelsea's knowledge of this unique project.

"I have to say, young lady," he began. "You know quite a bit about this process. Maybe someday you can work here. I'd love to see you in charge of projects like this."

Chelsea was considering work in cancer research, but now her focus was quickly swayed toward biomechanical engineering.

"That would be so cool," she replied.

Having had a brief look at what could be described as a Frankensteinian fantasy, the doctor informed her that staying any longer could create the risk of contamination.

As the doctor lead Chelsea back to the changing room, he told her about another related project.

"Did you know that we're also working on a similar project using asparagus?" he asked.

Chelsea gave his question a moment of thought.

"Yes," she replied. "Spinal cord injuries, right?"

The doctor was not so stunned this time and asked her to embellish on what she already knew. She explained the process in striking detail.

Doctor Stewart looked at her with great interest.

"Chelsea," he began. "When you get out of medical school, I want you to consider working here. We could use someone like you."

Chelsea was thrilled at the prospect of working on such high level projects and planned on consulting her counselor as soon as she returned to school.

Looking at his watch, Doctor Stewart noted the time and, turning to the teens, declared that it was time for lunch. Everyone was hungry and eager to get food in their stomachs.

"Alright," he said. "Let me show you where the cafeteria is. I have to go to a meeting, so after you get something to eat, feel free to wander around the campus. There's just one thing I want you to remember. If you see any signs that say anything about lethal force, don't go into those places. Those areas are under guard by military personnel, understand?"

It was at this point that the teens fully realized where they were and the nature of the work being done.

11

The group soon found themselves seated around a large table with trays of food in front of them. As they ate, they were surprised at how good it was.
"Holy shit," Kyle said. "I thought government food would suck, but this is really good."
In spite of his scientific genius, those who knew him in school tended to think of him as something of an asshole. He was arrogant and took great pleasure in playing pranks on people. Some of which were fairly cruel. But today he was far too involved in where he was to consider playing pranks and had become very aware of what the consequences could be. Not only had federal agents done background checks on everyone, but had also reviewed their school records in order to get a clear picture of their behavior. Although Kyle was one of the five who had won the lottery, allowing him to go on the tour, he was nearly excluded based on his behavior.

After lunch, they were allowed to wander the campus. However, it was insisted on that a security guard be assigned to them. As a matter of course, the guard was armed, and the teens noticed this right away. As they made their way around the campus, a multitude of questions flooded their minds. They were, however, allowed to take a few pictures but only in certain areas. The guard stated that this was strict policy and was for the benefit of national security. Those two words struck both fear and awe into the teens. Even Kate's mother was deeply affected and was careful about what the teens photographed. Hearing this, the voice of curiosity was heard.
"What would happen if we took pictures of something

we're not supposed to?"
John was the only one among them who was willing to ask what the others were thinking.
"Well," the guard began.
He spoke with a serious tone, but also with the intention of pranking all of them.
"First, if any of you compromise national security, we would take your phones and destroy them."
The teen's eyes widened with fear as they hung on every word.
"Then, according to federal law, you would be taken into custody and charged as spies. From there, it's just a matter of finding out who you're working for. Did that answer your question?"
The teens were mortified. Even Kate's mother seemed gravely concerned. Certainly, these things didn't really happen in the good old USA, right?

    The teens were brilliant in their chosen sciences, but knew nothing of the inner workings of their government. The idea that their rights could be circumvented or outright violated was something they had never considered. To be detained and possibly interrogated over a few pictures seemed, at least, outrageous. And as they stared at each other in shock, the guard, unable to suppress his laughter any longer, dropped his facade and confessed to a cruel sense of humor. Again, Kyle spoke up.
"You know something?" he asked.
"What's that?" the guard replied.
With a straight face, Kyle delivered an insult that, under the circumstances, was less than appropriate.
"You're a dick."
Kate's mother gasped in shock as the guard began laughing. The rest of the teens were too angry at the guard's choice of jokes to find any humor in it.

"Alright," he began. "We're not going to lock any of you up. Just be careful about where you go and what you take pictures of."
The guard brought them back to the elevator and as the doors closed, a tense silence flooded the air. Even the guard had become uncomfortable and secretly wished he had not played such a cruel joke on the teens.

They were led back down the first floor corridor and out through the glass double doors to a waiting van, where their driver sat in the front seat. Kate's mother, again, began to sweat as her face flushed a fiery red. Drawing closer to Kate, she continued to express her interest in him.
"Holy fuck," she whispered. "I hope I brought enough extra panties."
Kate's embarrassment was quickly turning to frustration as she whispered back in her mother's ear.
"Jesus fuckin' Christ, mom, will you knock it off?"
Her mother couldn't help but react with a slight sadistic grin, knowing how much her adult sense of humor bothered her. Turning towards Kate's ear again, she made one last remark.
"Well, I hope he's good at masonry because I've got a crack that needs filling."
Kate gave out a heavy sigh of frustration as she made her way into the van, sitting as far from her mother as possible. Most of the time, her mother was rather light-hearted, but occasionally and usually at the wrong time, she could be something of a handful – especially where men were concerned.

With everyone seated and belted in, the driver started the van and slowly pulled away from the curb. From there, he turned left and entered a traffic circle that led to the campus perimeter. It would be a long drive, but what it held in the store for the teens would be nothing short of remarkable. Kate's mother, of course, was continuing to flirt with the driver, who was trying his best to ignore her advances while focusing on the road. After a few miles, the driver directed the group's attention to a large clearing on the left. In the distance, was what looked like a tall, narrow tower. They were not allowed to get too close, but the driver managed to get a bit closer and then stopped. Prompting them to focus on the tower, the group noticed a white, elongated shape that seemed to be standing next to the tower.

"Holy shit!" Kate said. "Is that a rocket?"

Straining to see, the rest of the group soon realized that the enormous object was, indeed, a rocket. The driver soon provided the group with more information about its coming liftoff.

"I was asked to bring all of you out here, so you could this. I mean, you can't go to Nasa without seeing a liftoff, right?"

All eyes were fixed on the titanic structure standing in the distance as trails of nitrogen gas flowed down its side.

"So," John began. "What kind of rocket is this?"

Being more than familiar with rocket designs, Kate was quick to provide an answer.

"That's the Atlas 5. It's used to carry satellites into orbit. This is going to be so cool."

Turning to the driver, she asked if they could get out and watch. He thought about it only for a few moments and decided that the launch was far enough away that they could safely watch from outside the van.

"Okay," he answered. "But stay close to the van. Nobody wanders off, got it?"

They all agreed as they crowded out of the van, with one or two of them tumbling to the ground. The driver told them to be careful, but seeing their clumsiness brought a slight grin to his face. Later, he would entertain his co-workers with a narrative of the event. Elaine, however, was unable to contain her laughter and as the teens gathered at the side of the van, those few whose faces were covered with dirt looked back at her with a scolding expression. This was short-lived as a distant voice could be heard counting back from ten. But before the count-down was complete, a flash of light burst out from the tower's platform, followed by a fiery explosion as the rocket slowly pushed its way skyward. The group was struck with amazement by such a miracle of technology and speechlessly stared as it rose higher into the sky, a trail of fire following behind.

The experience seemed to last forever, but soon it was gone, as the rocket continued to push itself just beyond the edge of space. Once at its destination, it would deliver its payload and become another piece of space junk, drifting forever without purpose. Now, with their excitement having subsided, the teens had questions.
"So," John began. "What's in the rocket, a satellite?"
In spite of the driver's lack of knowledge, the group quickly looked to him for an answer.
"Well," he replied. "Even if I knew, I don't think I could tell you. There's a lot of classified projects going on here."
The teens were visibly disappointed but clearly understood the need for secrecy and after the last plume of steam vanished from the sky, they loaded themselves into the van and continued on their way around the campus' perimeter.

12

Before the van pulled up in front of the main building, the teens, having begun to feel the effects of the day's events, started to drift off. Although Elaine found herself fatigued as well, she managed to wake the group enough to inform them they were soon heading back to the hotel. This was met by weak groans and nodding heads. But they were soon brought back to life by the van's sudden stop as the driver pulled up in front of their hotel. Tomorrow would be day two of their tour but for now, the teens were in need of food and sleep and Elaine had already planned out their dinner. It was just a matter of dining in or out and given the condition of the group, she guessed that they would want to eat in their rooms. Plagued by the need for sleep, the teens ate their dinner, seemingly without realizing what they were eating. Some stayed up to watch a bit of TV, while the rest quickly went to sleep. By nine o'clock, everyone had fallen into a deep sleep, their bodies, and minds re-tuning for the next day's activities.

The next morning saw a repeat of the previous day. The teens were slow to rise, prompting Elaine to strongly suggest a return trip home if they didn't quicken their pace. Naturally, with the previous day's memories, the teens were eager to see more and rushed through their morning ritual with uncanny speed. Elaine was truly impressed by how five teenagers could move so quickly when they had a good reason for doing so.

13

Thirty minutes after opening their eyes, the group found themselves waiting outside for the driver. He was not expected to be late, but in their excitement the group lost track of time and just as they were to comment on the driver's tardiness they noticed a familiar white van approaching the hotel. The driver pulled over and, stopping in front of the hotel, heard the side door open as the teens climbed in. With Elaine in the front passenger seat, still fantasizing about the driver, they drove away and towards NASA's main campus. The teens wondered what technological leaps they would see today and with Doctor Stewart, once again, waiting near the front door, they quickly piled out and stood in an orderly manner. Doctor Stewart and Elaine were beyond surprised at how five teenagers could organize themselves with such speed.

Doctor Stewart, once again, directed the group down the hallway to the elevator. Stopping at the fifth floor, they stepped out and were guided down the corridor to a door at the end of the hallway. Now, it would be Kyle's turn to get up close to something he would never have dreamed seeing. Stopping at the door, Doctor Stewart turned to the group.
"Now, who is our nuclear chemist?"
All eyes turned to Kyle, who stammered his response.
"Uh, I guess that's me."
Doctor Stewart motioned him forward and opening the door hinted to him about the project being worked on.
"I've always thought of this project as being a bit other-

worldly."

Kyle's became more interested with every step, and soon he found himself in a changing room similar to where Chelsea had been yesterday. He was instructed to put a white clean suit on over his clothes with the last parts being a hood and face mask. After washing his hands, he put on a pair of latex gloves and was led into the lab.

"Now," Doctor Stewart began. "Take a good look around and tell me what you think they're working on."

Looking down the right side of the room, Kyle noticed a series of Plexiglas containers. A lab technician stood in front of each, dressed in a white, clean suit. In the center of each container was an irregularly shaped black object. They looked unfamiliar and unless Kyle could get closer, he would not know exactly what they were.

"So, what do you think?" Doctor Stewart asked.

Kyle strained to see the objects in more detail.

"I don't know," he replied.

Doctor Stewart motioned him towards the right side of the lab, closer to the plexiglass containers. In it was what looked like a rock with sharp jagged edges and a rather dull appearance.

"Go ahead," the doctor said.

Kyle moved closer as the technician was motioned away.

"Do you know what this is?"

In a sterile environment, Kyle suspected the black chunks were likely meteorites. But something was different about them. Meteorites were rarely black – usually gray or brown, depending on their composition.

"I'm not sure," he answered. "Meteorites?"

Doctor Stewart wanted him to think with the mind of an analytical chemist – a scientist.

"I don't think these come from that far away," he said.

"You're wearing gloves, right?"

Kyle held up his hands, displaying the protection he had

stretched over them earlier.

"Okay," the doctor continued. "Open those two ports and put your hands in."

Kyle nervously opened the ports and slowly put his hands through. He considered that the objects were likely rare, making him that much more anxious about being so close. Still, he was confused about what should have been obvious.

"I'm not sure," he said.

Doctor Stewart put a hand on top of the container as if to further point them out.

"Kyle," he said. "These are something that you will likely never see again. These are moon rocks."

Kyle was stunned and standing in front of these objects felt the blood leave his head. Doctor Stewart was correct. He would never see anything like this again.

Pausing for far too long, Kyle began to feel a bit weak in the knees, but recovered quickly as he asked a curious question.

"Can I touch it?"

Doctor Stewart gave it a moment's thought and decided that as long as Kyle keep his gloves on, it should be of no harm to allow him this rare opportunity.

"Okay," he replied. "But keep your gloves on. We can't risk contamination."

Kyle nodded his head as he reached in further. Touching the rock with a fingertip, he could feel its rough texture and sharp points. But his experience with non-terrestrial objects was brief, as the doctor tapped his shoulder and motioned him back to the changing room. Soon after, Kyle found himself back in the corridor. The teens noticed an odd look on his face and impatiently asked him what he had seen. He recovered himself enough to briefly describe his experience.

"You would not believe it. I got to touch an actual moon

rock. How cool is that?"
He took a moment to breathe out his excited tension as the others marveled at his once in a lifetime opportunity. Even Elaine was amazed. But it was time to move on and there was much more to see.

Once again, their guide led them back to the elevator and as they crowded in, John looked over at Kyle, whose face was still pale from an experience he would never have again.
"Hey, Kyle," John said. "You okay?"
Kyle responded with a slight stammer.
"Uh, yeah, fine."
Kyle and John were not exactly the best of friends, and occasionally butted heads over trivial matters. Among his less favorable qualities, Kyle tended to be a bully and took any opportunity to tease John for no other reason than the pleasure of doing so.

14

At Doctor Stewart's request, the group moved on and entering the elevator were taken to the fifth floor. Again, the corridor appeared as all the others – sterile and pale. Led away from the elevator, they made their way around a corner and stopped in front of a large window. Beyond this was a large lab with a second adjacent to it.
"Okay," Doctor Stewart began. "Who's our engineer?"
John immediately raised his hand, knowing it was his turn to be up close to another technological miracle.
"John, right?" Doctor Stewart asked.
John nodded his head as the doctor motioned him toward a nearby door. Once inside, he was told that there would be no need for a clean suit and that only the construction lab required such precautions.

The lab was sparsely staffed with the reasoning that these people were the planning team for this particular project. Scanning the area, John noticed a large black board covered with equations. As a promising engineering student, complex math was not only essential, but was also his specialty. The more complicated it was, the more he enjoyed working with it. He believed that mathematics was the language of the universe and that explanations for any phenomena could be gained through it. Perhaps the existence of God could someday be either proven or disproven through its use.

He asked the doctor if he could examine the equations more closely. The answer, of course, was yes, and as John moved up to the black board he recognized some of the variables as having to do with thrust – measured in Newtons. But the more he examined these equations, the more he realized that something was amiss. It was almost insignificant, but could make a huge difference if put into practice. Picking up a chalk erasure, he looked at one small piece of the numbers and letters that flowed across the board and began making what he believed to be a necessary change. But as the erasure touched the board, one of the scientists took a step forward as if to stop him. Doctor Stewart put out an arm, holding him back.

"Let him go," he said. "I want to see where this is going."
Within moments, John had made a correction that would have a profound impact on the device being built in the next room and with the rest of the group watching through the glass, he looked over at them and grinned slightly. Stepping aside, the staff, including Doctor Stewart, approached the board and studied the change John had made. They stood in amazement as each of them realized its meaning. Now, Doctor Stewart motioned John aside.

"Do you know what we're doing here?
John pointed to the room where construction on what appeared to be a spacecraft was underway.

"Well," John replied. "I'm pretty sure it has something to do with that satellite over there."

"That's right," the doctor said. "C'mon, let me give you a closer look."

Walking over to the window, John could see what was obviously a satellite.

"Now," the doctor continued. "I'm sure you've heard of near earth objects, right?"

"Oh, of course," John answered. "Those things fly by us all the time."

"Right," the doctor replied. "So we're going to send this up and crash it into a relatively small asteroid and see if we

can move it off course. The correction you made saved millions of dollars because had it not been for that correction, this satellite would have missed its target due to a thruster malfunction. What you did was brilliant."
Moving in closer, the doctor spoke quietly.
"And I think I may have to have a little talk with the chief scientist about this."
Breaking away from the conversation, John asked about the politics that might be associated with the project.
"Are other countries working on projects like this?"
The doctor nodded.
"As a matter of fact, there are several countries working jointly with us. These are countries also participating in the planetary defense policy. I guess everyone is afraid of the same thing."
John knew exactly what he meant and posed another question, one that caught the doctor off-guard.
"What if it doesn't work? Even smaller asteroids move really fast."
The doctor's face took on a grim expression.
"Well, we do have a contingency plan to launch at least one of our nukes at it. The problem is that nukes work the way they do partially by spreading across the ground. In space, you're not going to have that, so the detonation will take the form of a gigantic bubble. We just don't know if that's going to be enough, especially where the larger asteroids are concerned."

    John knew the consequences should the project fail, resulting in humankind being wiped from the planet. But he wondered if that would be such a bad thing. The problem with planet earth was not the planet. The problem was people, and without them the planet would have the chance to heal itself, as if humankind had never been there at all.
"I hope it works," John said.

Doctor Stewart hesitated as he considered the odds of success. Nothing is one hundred percent and the lab staff always tried to ignore the potential for the project's failure. Leaving the lab, John was met with the excitement of the group. Some of them knew the meaning of the change John made and congratulated him as if he had just saved the world. And in some small way, he may have done just that, but no one would be certain of its success until the mission was launched. Until then, fingers were crossed, and some lab staff resorted to prayer.

15

The group's excitement subsided quickly as Doctor Stewart led them down the corridor. Once again, they found themselves in the elevator and moving up two floors entered another sterile-looking corridor. Leading the group, the doctor stopped at a door that seemed different from the rest, bearing the number 9 fixed to its center. Everyone was curious about what might be behind the door, but it was Ethan who asked first.
"What's this room for? Another lab?"
All eyes turned to Doctor Stewart for an answer.
"This room isn't really a lab," he answered. "But we do conduct experiments in it."
He opened the door to a room lined with long triangular structures. This piqued the group's curiosity. All except for John. His background also covered audio engineering, and he was quick to point out that the objects lining both floors, walls and ceiling were baffles, designed to absorb sound. But what he was unable to figure out was what the room was specifically used for.
"So, what do you use this room for," he asked.
Doctor Stewart explained that more sensitive aircraft and satellite parts were tested for vibration using sound waves. A threshold was established for each item being tested. If the vibration of any object registered past this threshold, it would be considered failed and would have to be redesigned. But Ethan had one more question.
"What's the number nine for?"

The doctor no longer found himself surprised by any of

the questions put to him, as he had realized just how intelligent and knowledgeable the teens were.

"The sound level of this room has been measured at minus nine decibels. So we call it 'room nine'.

Ethan's knowledge of audio engineering was limited, but continued inquiring about the room's construction.

"I know this is going to sound weird, but has this room ever been used on a person?"

Such experiments were generally classified, but Doctor Stewart kept his response brief.

"We've found that exposure to this room can play tricks on a person's mind. If you're in there for more than a few minutes, you'll start hearing your heartbeat and the sound of your blood whooshing past your ears. A little more time and you'll be able to hear your internal organs moving – especially your intestines. From what I've heard, it can be a little creepy."

Kyle raised a hand, his curiosity getting the better of him.

"Yes," the doctor said.

"What would happen if someone stayed in there for, let's say, an hour?"

Doctor Stewart was quick with an answer but, again, kept it brief.

"From the studies we've done, we found that a prolonged time in this room can result in hallucinations, panic and aggressive behavior. Essentially, a reactive psychosis. It's both interesting to see what this level of sensory deprivation can do to the mind, but it can be dangerous to keep someone in there for too long."

Just before the group moved on, John asked if he could go into the room – just for a few moments.

"I understand the risk," he said. "But a few moments would be okay, right?"

Doctor Stewart agreed. After all, what harm could it do and as intelligent as the teens were he fully expected that one of them would want to go in. Opening the door, John stepped into the room and was struck by the symmetry of its construction. The baffles were made from acoustic tile and shaped into long, narrow pyramids. Even the backside of the door was covered with baffles, leaving no escape for any degree of sound. The room was fairly small and as John stood in the middle of it he began speaking.
"Hello."

He expected a small echo, but there was nothing, only the odd sound of his muffled voice. He wondered if the strange absence of an auditory response was real, or if it was a trick played on his mind by deprivation caused by the baffled walls. John quickly came to the conclusion, should he stay any longer, this sensation might take a more harmful turn and the idea of hallucinating made the experience even more uncomfortable.
"Well," he said. "That's enough of that."

Doctor Stewart continued holding the door open as John left the room. Physically trembling, he requested a glass of water and a quiet to sit, the sensory deprivation of room 9 had already taken something of a toll on his nerves. The rest of the group looked at him with obvious concern. Elaine was especially worried as she was the person chosen to be in charge of the teens as well as their safety.
"Holy shit," John said. "That was weird."
Doctor Stewart turned to him with a slight grin.
"No," he began. "I don't think you would."
Pausing in the corridor, John asked the doctor a curious question.
"As a matter of fact, I have." he answered.
"So, what happened?" John asked.

The doctor was quick with answer, as the experience had made a significant impact on his.

"I lasted about three minutes. I decided it was over when I starting hearing my mother's voice, and she's been dead for years."

The idea of a deceased relative speaking to someone while being locked in what is essentially a sensory deprivation room led John to feel both a noticeable degree of fear and anxiety.

Doctor Stewart studied his expression for a moment and seeing the tension on his face asked if he was alright.

"Yeah," John replied. "Just give me a few minutes."

The doctor, continuing his concern, motioned him to the wall and retrieving a chair from a nearby office asked John to sit.

"You take as much time as you need," he said.

Having drunk a second cup of water, John felt his nerves ease as he sat back in the chair, breathing deeply.

"Okay," he said. "I think I'm ready to go."

Standing up, he joined the rest of the group while the doctor led them down to the elevator.

Waiting for the doors to open, Doctor Stewart received a message on his pager, prompting him to walk to the nearest office to make what seemed to be an urgent call. Upon returning, he told the teens that there would be a delay in their tour but not wanting to abandon them, he decided to take them to someplace closer. This time, the group would go to an early lunch, then on to two more labs before calling it a day. Visiting this next lab would be brief, allowing the doctor time to attend whatever situation he was notified of.

"Okay," he began. "This next project is called the 'Lunar Flashlight'."

No one in the group had ever heard of such a device, and the doctor saw a lost, but curios look on the teens faces as one of them asked the obvious question.

"What does it do?"

The doctor's explanation was brief. However, driven by curiosity, John slipped away and quietly walked back to Room nine. Opening the door, he slipped in. As an engineering student, he was fascinated with its construction and again called out toward the walls, hearing nothing but the roar of silence. Studying its interior, he noticed a video camera placed high in a corner and assumed that whatever experiments were done had to be closely monitored. Naturally, there were no windows. He studied the details of the baffle's construction when he heard the door slam shut behind him, and as John walked over to it he heard the sound of the lock bolting shut. He tried to avoid panicking, knowing that there was also a lock on the inside. Turning the lock, he found that it refused to budge. He thought the lock could be jammed or there was something blocking the door. Either way, John was trapped and if he wasn't able to get out it wouldn't be long until he would begin to feel his faculties break down as he fell into an unrecoverable psychosis.

There was no point in trying to figure out how he had shut into what was, essentially, a sensory deprivation chamber. The important thing was that John dedicate as much energy as possible to getting out. Sitting on the floor, John tried to quiet his mind so as to be able to think clearly. But the time for mental clarity was running out, and he began to experience some of the things Doctor Stewart had mentioned. As he sat in the middle of the room, he began to hear the blood rushing past his ears. Soon after, he hears his intestinal tract groaning as it moved its contents along its predetermined path. Then, the trembling started, followed by the anxious shaking of his limbs. Fear was setting in and with that, panic. He was cognizant enough to realize that there were no options and until someone was able to open the door, John's sanity would continue to dwindle, leaving him in a state he could not begin to imagine.

16

Doctor Stewart called for someone to continue as the group's guide while he dealt with whatever it was that so quickly captured his attention over the phone. His replacement, Doctor Greer, knew nothing about the group or how many should be in attendance. He certainly didn't realize that one of them was missing. But moving forward, he formed his own itinerary and took the reminder of the group to some of the more interesting labs, those projects that involved far more complexity than what they had already seen. He wanted them to not just be interested but fascinated in the development of what some may call the 'technology of the future'.
"So," Doctor Greer began. "He showed you the Lunar Flashlight, huh?"
He let out a brief laugh as he explained its use.
"Do you know what that thing does? It allows you to see water on the lunar surface. Yeah, that's a big deal, right?"
He motioned the group through a maze of corridors.
"C'mon, I'll show you some real science."
The teens wondered if they weren't getting in over their heads and that maybe they might be exposed to something that shouldn't be seen. But with very little conversation between them, the group continued as their new guide began describing what they were about to see, and soon they found out just how talkative their new guide was. Still, no one had realized that one of them was missing.

17

While the rest of the group stood around a large quantum computer, John sat in the middle of the floor in room 9. It had been half an hour, and he had become nearly catatonic as his psyche began to disintegrate. But the worse was well on its way and promised to do far more damage than simply turning John into a statue. As he sat motionless, he could feel the heaviness of the surrounding silence. Soon, this would be replaced by a cacophony of voices screaming in his mind. Some he recognized – his mother and father. Others he believed to be the voice of God, telling him that he would soon die and cursing him for living a failed life. All reason had left John's otherwise brilliant mind as he was being reduced to a less than intelligent psychotic mute. But something inside him refused to break, and John up from the floor and began screaming while pounding on the baffles. No one would hear a sound.

Another hour had gone by and the inside of room nine was heavily stained with blood. John lay in the middle of the floor, his eyes wide open as saliva slowly ran from his mouth and onto the wood floor. If he were found soon, he might survive – physically. But mentally, his mind had turned to the consistency of mud. His brilliant intellect dissolved away, leaving him as an empty shell, with voices still running unceasingly through what was left of his mind. His sense of logic gone, John was functioning on what remained of his instincts, and as he stumbled to his feet began screaming again. But these were not the screams of someone trying to attract attention to an otherwise desperate circumstance. This was the shrieking of blind hysteria – a last futile attempt to survive. But the sound of terror went unheard and although there was a video camera mounted in the room, there was no one on the other end to rescue him.

18

The group, minus one, had moved on to another lab. They had become so engrossed in the science they were being introduced to that no one noticed John's absence. With a cafeteria nearby, their new guide gave them an hour to eat and relax. As they stood in line, it was Kate who noticed that they were one short of their group.
"Uh, guys," she said. "Where's John?"
They glanced around, hoping to see him somewhere in the cafeteria, but could not be found.
"Shit," Kate said. "Where did he go?"
Ethan spoke up with a concerned voice.
"Well, he couldn't have gone far, right?"
Kyle was next, but his concern seemed half-hearted.
"Can we eat first, then look for him?"
Kate became furious at his lack of concern.
"Kyle," she said. "Don't be an asshole. We'll eat later."
This brief exchange caught Elaine's attention, who approached the group with grave concern.
"What's going on, guys?" she asked.
Kate looked at her as Kyle looked away with an anxious expression.
"I think we lost John," she replied.
Elaine quickly went from concerned to frustrated.
"What do you mean, you lost John?"
Kate's voice began to stammer as she began to feel the pressure of a responsibility that was not hers. Her mother was there as chaperone and the responsibility for the teen's safety fell to her.
"Hey," Kate said. "This isn't my fault. You're supposed to be the one in charge."
In spite of Kate's angry words, her mother knew she was right and, taking a few minutes to calm herself, asked

where Doctor Greer was. The response from the group was silence. As the teens broke off for lunch, their new guide seemed to have vanished, and it was imperative that he be notified as quickly as possible.

19

Leaving the cafeteria, Kate took the lead and quickly found a security officer. Her words were frantic as she tried to organize her thoughts, but was interrupted by the security officer.
"Slow down," he began. "Now, what's wrong?"
She hesitated and taking a deep breath explained their situation to the officer.
"One of the people in our group is missing and…"
The security officer didn't need to hear anymore and, interrupting Kate, radioed to the campus security office. They, in turn, contacted Doctors Greer and Stewart. Once in attendance, the teens were asked to return to the cafeteria with the suggestion that they get something to eat. Wanting to help, Kate volunteered the group to help find John, but with so many classified projects being worked on, Doctor Stewart thought it best that they stay behind while a security team was organized to search the building.

However, in order to keep the group closely monitored, Doctor Greer suggested they get their lunch and eat in a more secure room where a guard could be placed outside. This only served to further raise their concerns.
"Don't worry," Doctor Stewart said. "We'll find him. These hallways can be like a maze, but the security guards know these buildings very well, okay?"
Kate knew that they had everything under control. But this did nothing to alleviate her mounting concern, feeling that something terrible had happened.

Having been escorted to a secure room, the teens ate

nervously, knowing a guard was standing just outside the door. The odds of being able to help in the search for their missing friend were about as good as being able to sneak past the guard. They would simply have to wait, and the security guard wasn't going anywhere.

    Led by Doctor's Greer and Stewart, the security team combed through the building, but it didn't take long to find John. The door of room 9 had been blocked shut by an office chair that had been jammed up under the door handle. Removing it, the door was opened to a scene of such horror that one of the security guards was forced to turn away as he vomited violently. By this time, John was dead.
"Jesus Christ," Doctor Stewart said. "How the fuck did this happen?"
Turning to the security guards, he gave an angry order.
"I want to know who the fuck did this. Bring them to my office, now!"
Doctor Greer spoke up with a question.
"What about the other kids? What do we tell them?"
Wiping the sweat from his forehead, Doctor Stewart hesitated.
"We can't let this get out of the building," he said. "This could be a public relations nightmare. Plus, the director would have my ass. Shit, this could go all the way to the President."
Never having dealt with anything like this, he decided that the CIA should be brought in. If the situation called for extreme measures, they could come up with a solution and with an office nearby, it wouldn't be long before their arrival.

20

A call was made over a secure line and within minutes two agents appeared in the hallway. Both dressed in black suits and sunglasses. Doctor Stewart was certain they were armed as well. They stood motionless outside the entrance of room 9, examining the gruesome scene within.
"I don't know this could have happened but…"
One of the agents cut him off mid-sentence.
"Sir," he began. "It doesn't matter how it happened. What has to be done is something you will not be involved in."
Before the crowd was dismissed, the agents were informed that the deceased teenager was part of a small tour group. It was made clear they could never be told of what had happened, nor could they be allowed to leave for fear that there would be questions pertaining to their missing friend. The only question was how to go about eliminating what might be seen as a national security threat, or at least an incident that might reflect badly on the current administration.

While the agents considered several ideas, Doctors Stewart and Greer approached them with a plan. The agents, again, reiterated that they had everything under control but the two men insisted on conveying their idea.
"I know this is what you guys do," Doctor Stewart said. "But we have this experimental aircraft. It's flown remotely and it might be the solution you're looking for."
The agent, who did not share his name, suggested the conversation continue in private. Doctor Stewart agreed and, turning to Doctor Greer, asked him to return to his office. The fewer people involved, the better.

Retreating to a small conference room, Doctor Stewart offered a solution that, if carried out, would eliminate any political issues.

"Alright," he began. "This is going to sound a bit… inhuman, but I propose that we load the rest of these kids into that aircraft and… well...."

The agents looked at each other and nodded their agreement.

"Are you sure you don't want to go into the CIA?" one of them asked.

Doctor Stewart gave their question only a moment's thought.

"I think I'm fine where I am," he replied.

"Okay," the agent said. "We'll handle it from here. Just get those kids on that plane."

In spite of knowing that this had to be done, Doctor Stewart felt the sting of immorality stabbing at his conscience as he began to second guess himself. But he knew there was no other way to deal with what could explode into a media circus, possibly compromising the office of the presidency. There was simply no other way.

21

The first thing that needed to be done was to remove John's body, making sure he was, in fact, dead. CIA agents are thoroughly trained in many areas and were more than able to declare a death. Even if John wasn't dead, he soon would be, and his body would quickly be transported off-site for incineration. Room 9 would also need cleaning. Whatever surfaces were deeply stained would be sanded down. Any evidence of this incident had to disappear and anyone involved needed to be debriefed and sworn to secrecy in writing with the understanding that revealing what was now classified could result in federal charges.

During this process, the rest of the tour group was retrieved and directed away from the cleanup of room 9 towards a different elevator so as not to witness the gruesome fate of their now deceased friend. Doctor Stewart noticed the confused and fearful on their faces and offered a few calm words.
"Try not to worry, everyone. We'll find him. This is a pretty big place, and it's going to take some time."
This did little good to relieve the tension that fear often creates and while Kate's eyes began to tear up, Kyle started to feel faint as guilt quietly settled in on his conscience. Something told him that his actions may have ended with tragedy, but he didn't dare reveal that he was the one responsible.

Doctor Stewart forced a smile to his face as he announced where the group was going next.
"Okay, everyone, we have developed an experimental

aircraft. It's sitting in a hanger about a mile away, and I want all of you to see it."

As they exited the elevator, Kate raised a hand. "Shouldn't something like this be classified? I mean, if it's experimental…"

Doctor Stewart interrupted her with assurance that it was designed for high altitude flight and would not be used by the military. Kate, as well as the others, seemed satisfied with his explanation, but still, in the back of their minds, each knew there was something more than what Doctor Stewart was telling them.

Loaded back into the van, Doctor Stewart told the driver to take the group to hanger two. Following this order without question, he began the mile-long drive to NASA's flight line. Stopping at hanger two, they were met by the research team's director. Minutes ago, he had received a call from the CIA agents responsible for the containment of the incident about to unfold and would be there momentarily. The teens were not allowed to go into the hangar, but the aircraft would soon be towed out to them. Kate's mouth dropped open as the aircraft emerged into the midday sun. As a designer, she saw it as a grand thing of beauty – a work of technological art. Beyond this, none of the group had any idea of the reason they were really there.

With Doctor Stewart standing in the background, the director of the project began a brief presentation on the aircraft's capabilities, designed specifically for high altitude flight near the edge of the mesosphere. At this altitude, sprites, and stars could be easily seen as well as the earth below. The only other person who seemed to be impressed was Ethan, whose eyes lit up as the aircraft's engines began to start, with a loud whine turning into a deafening roar. The project's director signaled the pilot to shut down the engines and was quiet again, he turned to the group and explained a few more of the aircraft's features. He spoke for no longer than five minutes, then asked the teens if they wanted to see the inside. The response was an overwhelming yes.

Once the hatch was opened, the teens, including Elaine, were shown in and directed to the rows of seats lining both sides of the cabin. Its interior looked more like a private jet, and Ethan guessed that this might be an alternative means of transportation for the President, given the altitude it was capable of. He asked the director about this assumption, but due to the classified nature of the project, he could neither confirm nor deny it. Now, Kate spoke up with a question.
"Excuse me, I know this is a stupid question, but would it be okay if we took a ride in this?"
The director already knew what the answer would be, having become a willing participant in the creation of one incident meant to hide another.
"Well," he began. "I don't see why not, as long as it's a brief flight."
The group was ecstatic and instinctively fastened their seat-belts. Everyone was excited except for Kyle, who remained uncomfortably quiet throughout the conversation.

The pilot was ordered to exit the aircraft. Its interior design was such that he was able to leave without the teens noticing. Between this and their excitement, the group never suspected that anything was amiss and, assuming the pilot was still in the cockpit, held a great deal of trust in his abilities. The engines began to whine as they spun up to take off speed, and soon the aircraft filled with exuberant teenagers roared down the runway and gracefully rose from the tarmac. It seemed that within seconds, the aircraft had reached thirty thousand feet and was still climbing. Soon, the teens were able to see the curvature of the earth, as well as the division between daylight and the edge of space. All eyes were aimed out of the windows as the teens marveled at the view of what they knew was a once in a lifetime experience.

Back at hanger two, the pilot had already left. He was scheduled to test an aircraft designed for high altitude surveillance and knew nothing of what had been planned for the teens and their chaperone. Meanwhile, in a small room under the hanger, a man dressed in military fatigues sat at a console, gently moving a steering mechanism while staring at a display. Momentarily, another man walked in and stood behind him, studying the images drifting across the screen. Now, one of the CIA agents tapped the remote pilot on the shoulder.
"Yes, sir," the pilot said.
He turned slightly to a man dressed in a black suit, wearing sunglasses and displaying the obvious lump under his left arm, denoting the presence of a gun.
"Sargent," he began. "You're relieved."
The Sargent turned and looked at the agent as if he had lost his mind.
"But, I....."
His words were interrupted by the director, who pointed a thumb toward the door.
The Sargent, following his orders, put the aircraft on autopilot before rising from his seat. The agent immediately sat and took control of the aircraft, knowing exactly what had to be done. It was all a question of where the target would be.

Moments after taking the aircraft out of autopilot, he was handed a piece of paper displaying two sets of numbers. The agent glanced at them and nodded as they were placed on the console in front of him. Moving the control stick, he gently banked the aircraft left while reducing its altitude. Handing the paper to his well-dressed colleague, he instructed him to enter them into a targeting program. No sooner was this done than the radar displayed the numbers as a heading. The aircraft would now follow an imaginary path to the mark, displaying itself as a flashing green dot.

In the cabin, everyone felt the plane bank. It was a feeling none of them were used to, but they all took a few deep breaths as they tried to steady their nerves. A few moments later, they were, once again, at the windows looking out on the beauty of mother earth. As the plane dropped into heavier air, turbulence began shaking it, causing the teen's teeth to rattle slightly. Panic soon set in. Ethan was the first to express his anxiety.
"Guys, something's wrong. No plane should do this. I'm going to talk to the pilot."
Getting up from his seat, he went to the cockpit door as the plane continued shaking and knocked firmly. With no answer, he continued knocking, then pounding. Still, there was no answer.
"Someone's gotta be in there," he said.
Now, Chelsea got up from her seat and walking down the aisle also began pounding on the cockpit door. With no answer, they began yelling for the pilot to respond. But their words went unheard. Frustration was quickly building into anger as Ethan began throwing his shoulder into the door.
"God fuckin' damn. I swear I'm gonna break this thing down."
The plane continued shaking violently and as Ethan's anger mounted, so too did the force of his shoulder as the door's

latch suddenly gave way.

Having flung the door open, Ethan stood in the cockpit. His face had turned a deathly pale as panic overtook his senses.
"Guys," he began. "I think we've got a problem."
Getting to their feet, everyone went to the door of the cockpit. They saw an array of lights -- some flashing, some steady. But the one thing that was absent was a pilot, leaving the controls to drift around on their own.
"Jesus Christ," Chelsea said. "They're flying this remotely."
Panic turned to terror as the group began to wonder if the plane's structure was about to fail. They all had bright futures ahead of them and were looking forward to the challenge of higher education. Now, they felt as though their dreams had evaporated as the plane began to nose down.
"There's gotta be something we can do," Elaine said. "You guys are geniuses. Can't you think of something?"
A silent response flooded the cockpit when Ethan was struck with an idea. It was so simple and with enough strength, they might have a chance to, at least, gain control of the aircraft.
"Alright," Ethan said. "Everyone move back. I got an idea."
Sitting in the pilot's seat, he grabbed the steering mechanism and pulled. At first, the nose of the plane began to come up. Then, it began to fight back, as if someone on the other end was pushing it forward. Ethan pulled back again, but was met with a degree of force greater than his own strength. He sat back in the seat. His muscles ached as his skin broke into a fierce sweat. He had all but given up.
"Anybody else got any ideas?" he asked.
Again, silence.

The situation seemed dire and realizing that they were likely out of options, Kate retreated to the arms of her mother and burst into tears. The unavoidable had finally descended upon them, and none of them knew why. Even if Kyle had come forward with the responsibility of ending John's life, it certainly would have been of no use, and decided that revealing this could likely make things worse. He wondered if there were parachutes on-board. But after a few moments of thought, he came to the conclusion that even if there were enough, opening a parachute at this altitude and speed would cause it to shred, and they would die anyway.

Ethan was out of ideas and had personally resolved himself to the reality of his impending death. He sat in the pilot's seat, his mind frozen, insulated from the trauma they were about to dive into. The rest of the group sat on the floor; some crying hysterically, while others rocked back and forth, wide-eyed and catatonic. Their lives brushed away; their deaths relegated to a folder hidden in a vault marked 'classified'. No one would know what happened. Their families, as well as the public, were to be told about a tragic accident that took the lives of five brilliant teenagers, all on their way up in the world. Of course, Elaine's family, like the rest, could look forward to receiving a letter from a little-known agency of the government announcing the loss of their loved one – with condolences, naturally.

23

    The Blue Ridge Mountains were beautiful no matter what the season. But on one particular day, the serenity of what could easily be compared to as heaven was disturbed by a silver-white streak blazing down from a royal blue sky. Anyone in the area would have heard a loud boom, followed by the rumbling of an explosion as an unseen wave marched across the earth. Had there been eyes to witness the sight, they would have seen a white jet fall out of the sky, its engines still thundering, stopping upon impact. The cries of those inside would not be heard over the prolonged scream of the experimental aircraft just before colliding with its intended target, sending up plumes of smoke and debris. Everything in the cabin was incinerated as the fumes from its fuel tanks violently combusted. Any onlooker standing close enough, might have become blind or burned from the brilliant flash that scorched the earth, taking the lives of one adult and four teenagers.

22

The control room beneath hanger two had fallen silent with the realization that the plan to achieve political insulation had been far more successful than hoped for. The CIA agents work was finished, and they left the room without a word. No doubt, their job is one largely without morality, dedicated solely to the maintaining of power through secrecy. Doctor Stewart, on the other hand, was not so accustomed to this type of thinking, but did his best to bring a close to the events of the day.

"Okay," he began. "Contact the FBI. They'll handle it from here."

His specialty was science, not clandestine operations, cover stories or the taking of human life. As he stood in front of the control console, he thought there should be something more, something that could be said of the young lives he had, only hours ago, praised for their genius. But there was nothing. No words would be sufficient to honor those who died for nothing more than politics.

Still standing in the control room, he began to feel soiled by his participation in such a senseless act. Certainly, there could have been another way. But it was time to get back to his office, as the call of the mundane duties of his job whispered in his ear. Finally, before leaving the control room, he turned to the project director.

"Hey, do you know where the chapel is?"

End

www.ingramcontent.com/pod-product-compliance
Lightning Source LLC
LaVergne TN
LVHW051958060526
838201LV00059B/3709